CLEVER CAKES

"Rosen's inventiveness and manic style should present no problems for beginner readers with a sense of humour."
Tony Bradman, The Daily Telegraph

Michael Rosen is a popular author and performer, and the presenter of BBC Radio's children's book programme, Treasure Islands. His Walker books include *We're Going on a Bear Hunt* (winner of the 1989 Smarties Book Prize), *The Wicked Tricks of Till Owlyglass* (shortlisted for the 1989 Emil Award), four Scrapbooks (illustrated by Quentin Blake), *The Horribles* and *Little Rabbit Foo Foo*.

Caroline Holden has illustrated numerous children's books, including *The Secret Diary of Adrian Mole aged 13¾* and the Walker titles *Roseanne and the Magic Mirror* and *The Human Zoo* (both by Virginia Ironside).

*Giant Gobbleguts lived in a cave
near the village of No.*

CLEVER CAKES

Written by
MICHAEL ROSEN

Illustrated by
CAROLINE HOLDEN

WALKER BOOKS
LONDON

For Geraldine, Joe, Naomi,
Eddie, Laura and Isaac

First published 1991 by
Walker Books Ltd, 87 Vauxhall Walk
London SE11 5HJ

Text © 1991 Michael Rosen
Illustrations © 1991 Caroline Holden

Printed and bound in Great Britain by
Richard Clay Ltd, Bungay, Suffolk

British Library Cataloguing in Publication Data
A catalogue record for this book is available

from the British Library
ISBN 0-7445-2097-5

CONTENTS

Masha waited and waited
but they never came.

CLEVER CAKES

Once there was a girl called Masha who lived with her granny at the edge of the woods.

One day Masha said, "Granny, can I play outside with my friends?"

"Yes, Masha," said Granny, "but don't wander off into the woods, will you? There are dangerous animals there that bite..."

Off went Masha to play with her friends. They played hide-and-seek. Masha went away to hide and she hid right deep in the woods. Then she waited for her friends to find her. She waited and waited but they never came. So Masha came out of her hiding-place and started to walk home. She walked this way, then that way, but very soon she knew she was lost.

"He-e-e-lp!" she shouted. "He-e-e-e-lp!"

But no one came.

Then very suddenly up came a massive muscly bear.

"Ah hah!" said the bear. "You come with me, little girl. I'm taking you home. I want you to cook my dinner, wash my trousers and scrub the floor in my house."

"I don't want to do that or anything like it, thank you very much," said Masha. "I want to go home."

"Oh no you don't," said the bear. "You're coming home with me." And he picked up Masha in his massive muscly paws and took her off to his house.

So now Masha had to cook and clean and wash and dust all day long. And she hated

Masha had to cook and clean
and wash and dust all day long.

it. And she hated the massive muscly bear. So she made a plan.

She cooked some cakes, and then she said to the bear, "Mr Bear, do you think I could take some cakes to my granny?"

I'm not falling for a stupid trick like that, thought the bear. If I let her go to her granny's, she'll never come back.

"No you can't," he said. "I'll take your cakes to her myself."

And he thought, I'll eat all those cakes. Yum, yum, and yum again.

"Right," said Masha, "I'll put the cakes in this basket. Don't eat them on the way to Granny's, will you? Cos if you do, something terrible will happen to you."

"Of course I won't eat the cakes," said the bear.

As soon as the bear's back was turned, Masha jumped into the basket. When he turned round, he picked up the basket and walked off.

After a while, the bear got tired – ooh, that basket was so heavy, it was pulling off his arm – so he sat down.

"Now for the cakes," he said.

But Masha called out from inside the basket, "Don't you eat us, Mr Bear. We're little cakes for Masha's granny."

You should have seen that bear jump!

"The cakes heard me. Oh, yes, Masha did say if I ate them something terrible would happen to me. I'd better leave them alone."

So up got the bear and walked on … and on … and on … until he began to feel hungry. He thought, if I could eat the cakes without them knowing, surely nothing terrible will happen to me. But how can I eat them without them knowing? Then he said out loud, "Oooh, I wonder if those

11

little cakes would like to hop out of the basket and come for a walk with me."

But Masha called out from inside the basket, "Don't you dare touch us, you great greedy glut. We're little cakes for Masha's granny."

The bear nearly jumped out of his jacket.

"Woo-hoo, those devilish little cakes knew that was a trick. What clever cakes. Next time I won't say anything at all. I'll just sit down and gobble them up. Yum, yum, and yum again."

So up he got and walked on … and on … and on…

But now the bear was getting really very, very hungry. It felt like there was a huge hole in his belly. This time he remembered not to speak. Very carefully he sat down, and slo-o-o-o-wly he reached out his massive muscly paw for the basket. But

*Slo-o-o-o-wly the bear reached out
his massive muscly paw for the basket.*

Masha, peeking through the holes in the basket, could see what the bear was up to and she called out, "Don't you dare touch us, you horrible great greedy glut. We're little cakes for Masha's granny and if you touch us, we'll jump out of the basket faster than you can blink, and we'll eat you up, ears and all."

"Zoo-wow, those cakes must be magic!" said the bear. "I'd be crazy to touch them. I'd better take them to Masha's granny as quickly as I can or something terrible will happen to me." And he hurried on to Granny's house.

When he got there he shouted, "Open the door, Granny!"

Granny came to the door and when she saw a great big bear standing there she was scared stiff.

But little Masha called out from the

basket, "Look out, Bear, your time's up. Now we're going to eat you."

Bear dropped the basket, turned, and ran off shouting, "Help, help, the cakes are going to eat me, the cakes are going to eat me!"

As soon as the bear was off and away, out of the basket popped Masha. Oh, how pleased Granny was to see her, and how pleased Masha was to see her granny! They hugged and kissed each other so many times that there were no kisses left till the next day.

"What a clever girl you are, to trick that big bear," said Granny.

"Never mind that," said Masha. "Let's get these cakes inside us."

And that's what they did. Yum, yum, and yum again!

*Cherry-Berry's dad went out at night,
leaving her all alone in the house.*

CHERRY-BERRY

Cherry-Berry lived with her dad. Her mum had died some time before and ever since then things hadn't gone very well. Dad had changed. He'd become sad and hopeless and didn't look after her properly. He went out at night, leaving her all alone in the house. Cherry-Berry missed her mum and wanted her to come alive again. She kept a picture of her by the side of her bed, and she always remembered something that her mother had told her: One is weak, many are strong. She wasn't sure she knew what it meant but she liked the sound of it.

One night, her dad was out playing cards

with his friends in a little house at the edge of town. This night, like most nights, he was losing. Try as he might, he couldn't win and he was losing money again and again. He kept saying to himself, "If I could win just once, I'd go home. If only I could win just once – that's all I ask."

Then, faster than it takes to swallow a baked bean, a little knobbly man put his head round the corner and said to Cherry-Berry's dad, "You can win all the money you want if you do something for me."

"And what is it I'd have to do for you?"

"You must give me the first thing you speak of when you get home," said the little knobbly man.

"Well, that's easily done," said Cherry-Berry's dad. He thought how he could walk in at home and say, "I fancy a nice fresh slice of bread," or "Are we short of carrots?" and then he could give the little knobbly man a slice of bread or some carrots.

"Yes," said Cherry-Berry's dad, "that's easily done."

"Do you promise on the stars?" said the little knobbly man.

"I promise," said Cherry-Berry's dad. "Now let's get on with the game. I want to win."

So, Cherry-Berry's dad sat down at the table and, sure enough, he won. And he went on winning till the others wouldn't play any more. Now he had more money in his hand than he had seen in years and he went home a happy man.

"Cherry-Berry!" her dad called out. "We have money, my girl, no more worries."

The moment he said it, he clapped his hand over his mouth, but it was too late to stop the word coming out. He'd said it now.

"Little man, little man, where are you?"
called out Cherry-Berry's dad.

"What's the matter?" asked Cherry-Berry. She was well used to his strange and reckless ways. "Is something wrong?"

"Yes," said her dad. "I've done something terrible. A little knobbly man said he could help me win at cards if I gave him the first thing I spoke of when I got home. And the first thing I said was your name, Cherry-Berry."

"I'll have to think of something," said Cherry-Berry, and she took herself to bed.

In the morning Cherry-Berry said to her father, "Tell the little knobbly man that the first thing you spoke of was Cherry-Berry – it's a girl, and she'll be coming in a red dress."

So off went Cherry-Berry's dad to the little house at the edge of town, and he called out, "Little man, little man, where are you?"

And a voice came from the house, "I'm here, what will you bring me?"

"Cherry-Berry," said Cherry-Berry's dad.

"And how will I know this Cherry-Berry?"

"She's a girl and she'll be wearing a red dress."

Meanwhile, Cherry-Berry went off to school to find her friends.

"Listen," she said, "you've got to help me. When morning school's over, run home, change into red dresses and come with me to the edge of town."

And that's what they did.

Just before twelve o'clock a long line of girls in red dresses made their way to the house at the edge of town. Suddenly the little knobbly man appeared and said, "Where is Cherry-Berry?"

"I am Cherry-Berry," said the first girl.

"I am Cherry-Berry," said the second girl.

"I am Cherry-Berry," said the third girl. And so on through all the girls.

"BAH!" shouted the little knobbly man. He rushed away shouting, "You won't get away with this, you won't get away with this."

Cherry-Berry went home and when her dad got in later he was delighted to see her.

"Listen, Dad," said Cherry-Berry, "you may see the little knobbly man again. If you do, tell him I will come and I'll be wearing a white dress."

"Oh no," said her dad. "I'm not going back there again. I'm staying here to look after you."

But that night, after Cherry-Berry had gone to bed, once again he went off to play cards with his friends in the little house at the edge of town. But no sooner had he sat down at the table to play than out popped

"Who is Cherry Berry?"

the little knobbly man.

"Why did you play that trick on me?" he shouted.

"I did just as you told me to," said Cherry-Berry's dad.

"Make sure she comes tomorrow," said the little knobbly man. "How will I know it's her?"

"She'll be wearing a white dress," said Cherry-Berry's dad.

"And she'd better be, or you will be struck down dead."

In the morning Cherry-Berry's dad had to tell her what had happened.

So later, Cherry-Berry and her friends made their way to the edge of town dressed in white.

Out came the little knobbly man again. "Who is Cherry-Berry?"

"I am Cherry-Berry," said the first girl.

"I am Cherry-Berry," said the second girl.

"I am Cherry-Berry," said the third girl. And so on through all the girls.

The little knobbly man roared with anger. "You won't get away with this," he said, "you won't get away with this!" and disappeared.

Cherry-Berry went home and when her dad got in he was delighted to see her.

"Listen, Dad," said Cherry-Berry, "you may see the little knobbly man again. If you do, tell him I'll be wearing a black dress."

"Oh no," said her dad. "I'm not going back there again. I'm staying here to look after you."

But that night, after Cherry-Berry had gone to bed, once again he went off to play cards with his friends in the little house at the edge of town. No sooner had he sat down at the table to play than out popped the little knobbly man.

"Why did you play that trick on me?" he shouted.

"I did just as you told me to," said Cherry-Berry's dad.

"Make sure she comes tomorrow," said the little knobbly man. "How will I know it's her?"

"She'll be wearing a black dress," said Cherry-Berry's dad.

"And she'd better be, or your house will fall down with you in it."

In the morning, Cherry-Berry's dad had to tell Cherry-Berry what had happened.

But this time Cherry-Berry and her friends didn't go to the house at the edge of town. The little knobbly man waited and waited for her there, and when she didn't come he rushed down the road with a face like thunder.

*In rushed the little knobbly man and
down he fell into the cellar.*

"They won't get away with this," he shrieked. And when he got to Cherry-Berry's house he shouted, "Come out, come out, I want what was promised me."

But there was no answer.

"Right, I'm coming in!"

And in he rushed.

But Cherry-Berry and her friends had opened the door in the floor that led down to the cellar. In rushed the little knobbly man and down he fell into the cellar and Cherry-Berry slammed the door shut after him. The little knobbly man was locked tight in the cellar.

"Let me out! Let me out!" shouted the little knobbly man.

"Oh no," said Cherry-Berry. "Not you nor anyone like you."

When her dad came home later, he was delighted to see her.

"I didn't go to the little knobbly man this time, Dad," she said.

"And what happened?"

"He came here. He was angry because he couldn't have what you promised him."

"So then what happened?"

"Well, I was angry because you promised him something you should never have promised."

"So?"

"He's in the cellar."

"How did he get there?"

"We put him there."

So Cherry-Berry and her dad collected up all their things and ran out of the house. The last thing they heard was the little knobbly man shouting, "Right, your house will fall down with you in it!"

There was a crack, and a rumble, and a roar, and the house fell down and no one ever saw the little knobbly man again.

"Now we can go somewhere else to live," said Cherry-Berry, "and start a new life there."

"You're right," said her father, and he promised he'd never go back to the little house at the edge of the town again. And he didn't.

Cherry-Berry and her father lived together happily in their new home, and Cherry-Berry would often look at the picture of her mother by the side of her bed and think of her mother's old saying: One is weak, many are strong.

The Ding-a-ling Brothers were singing their song.

THE GREAT GOLDEN
BELLY-BUTTON

King Jabber sat listening to the concert. The Ding-a-ling Brothers were singing their song, "If I was a pudding, I'd ask you to be the custard". Oh dear, it was the thirty-ninth time he'd heard it and he hadn't liked it the first time. Yawn, yawn, yawn.

Then Donk the jester came on and told jokes. They were all terrible – especially the long one about the pig that ate the king's underpants.

When Wizzo the wizard stood on the stage and said that he was going to take a rabbit and a donkey out of his hat, enough was enough. King Jabber stood up and said, "I can't stand any more of this rubbish. I want fun, I want laughter, I want … I want … egg on toast."

The entertainers hurried off the stage and Bradstock brought in the egg on toast. The toast was soggy. The egg was burnt. Or was it the other way round?

"I'm supposed to be the king around here," said Jabber. "I'm royal and regal and you're loyal and legal. I'm supposed to sit about and do nothing all day, you're supposed to be really glad you've got a king, even though I cost an enormous amount of money, and we're all supposed to be terribly, terribly happy. But what happens? I'm bored and the Ding-a-ling Brothers are still singing that stupid song about the pudding and the custard. What am I going to do, Bradstock?"

"First of all, sir, can I suggest that you wipe the egg off your chin? And then might

"First of all, sir, can I suggest that you wipe the egg off your chin?"

I remind you, sir, of the Great Golden Belly-button you had made?"

"Yes, yes, yes, Bradstock. I do remember. What of it?"

"Well, sir," said Bradstock, "you don't seem to have found much use for it yet."

"Use? Use? You don't use a Great Golden Belly-button. It just is. I had it made because it's a good sight more fun than listening to Wizzo, Donk and the Ding-a-lings."

"I understand, sir," said Bradstock, "but I would like to suggest that you give it away, as a kind of prize. Whoever can make you laugh the most, will win the Great Golden Belly-button."

"No, Bradstock, anyone can make me laugh. It's too easy. I've got a better idea. Whoever can tell the biggest lie will win the Great Golden Belly-button. How about that?"

"Excellent idea, sir!"

So the herald went out all around the country telling people: "Hear this! Hear this! Whoever can show themselves to be the biggest liar in all the land will receive the Great Golden Belly-button from the hands of King Jabber himself."

It wasn't long before the palace was packed with people telling lies.

There was the woman who said she had a horse that could say, "sausages"; the man who said he had grass growing in his armpits; the woman who said she could swallow armchairs, and so on and so on.

Once again, King Jabber was getting bored.

"It's time we ended this stupid game of yours, Bradstock."

"Your stupid game, sir."

"Yours!"

"Yours!"

"Yours!"

Just then a voice piped up, "I'm here."

Bradstock and King Jabber looked round, and there stood a small girl with a bowl in her hand.

"Who are you?" asked the king.

"Oh, come on," said the girl, whose name was Peggy. "You remember me, don't you? You owe me a hundred gold pieces. I've come to collect them in my bowl here. It did have cornflakes in, but it's clean now. "

"A hundred gold pieces? A hundred gold pieces?" said the king. "I've never seen you before in my life. I've never promised you any money and you're a liar to say I have."

"You promised. You did!"

"Did you hear that, Bradstock? Have you ever heard a liar like this little sprat? Get out

38

"You owe me a hundred gold pieces," said Peggy.
"I've come to collect them in my bowl here."

of here, girl, before I set my dogs on you."

"Just hold it right there," said Peggy. "If you've never heard a liar like me before, then you must give me the Great Golden Belly-button."

"Ah. Er, well. Er, no..." said the king. "Of course I didn't mean you were really a liar, I, er..."

"Oh well, if I'm not a liar then give me my hundred pieces of gold," said Peggy.

There was silence. Bradstock waited to be given the order to set the dogs on her.

"Well sock me sideways, the little sprat has done it!" said King Jabber. "Girl, the Great Golden Belly-button is yours. Give it to her, Bradstock."

Bradstock gave Peggy the Belly-button and she left the palace with it in her breakfast bowl.

"Stupid game you thought up there,"

said the king to Bradstock.

"Stupid game *you* thought up, sir," said Bradstock.

"No, *you* thought up."

"No, *you* thought up."

"*You* thought up."

"More egg on toast, sir?"

"I suppose so," said the king.

*Desmond was stiff with cold
and nearly asleep on his feet.*

THE DEVIL-DOG

"I'm not afraid of the dark," said Desmond to himself. "I'm not afraid of the dark. Anyway, I ought to be used to it by now."

He was Farmer Fidler's boy on the farm up the valley and quite often he was kept working late. This night it was lambing – standing with the sheep trying to make sure every lamb that was in a mother ewe came out alive. He had gone on working till he was stiff with cold and nearly asleep on his feet. One moment he thought he saw a lamb with a dog's head, and the next he was sure he felt something strange in his hand, opened his fingers and there, looking at him, was what he thought was a big sheep's eye.

Now it was time for the walk home in the dark. No harm could come to him on the road, surely? There was the old beech tree – that meant he was half-way home. What if it *had* been a sheep's eye, he thought. What would I have done then? He shivered. What a cold night.

"What's that noise?"

There was a hard, brisk rustling in a tree above his head. He looked up. Nothing. Just the lines of the branches cutting up the sky.

He walked on. The cold was biting his face. He was coming to the bit of the road he called The Tunnel. Prickly hawthorn trees had grown over the road and any light from the moon or the stars was kept out by the branches. It was just like a tunnel. Desmond listened to the sound of his feet slow down as he stepped into it.

Well into the middle, he felt something

Desmond was coming to the bit
of the road he called The Tunnel.

on his neck. He rushed his hand up to it.

"What's that?" he screeched.

As he spoke, there was a rustle in the ditch beside him and he stopped dead still in the middle of the road. The thing on his neck was just a wet leaf, so that was that, but what was the rustle?

He looked into the deep dark of the ditch. There was more rustling and then a whimper. It sounded like a dog. A dog in pain. Desmond couldn't see, but he called out to it, "Here boy, here boy."

The thing whimpered again so he took a step nearer. He saw a flash of teeth and it rustled again. Was it a dog? Or something bigger? It seemed to be caught, helpless, so he stepped up to it.

Yes, it was a dog. Thank goodness for that! And it looked like it had broken its leg, poor thing, and had got weak and cold trying to get home. Mind you, whose dog was it? Desmond reckoned to know every dog round these parts and this red and white fellow wasn't one he recognized.

"Now, lie there a bit more, boy," he said to it, "and I'll fetch you some dock leaves from by the stream."

He had it in mind to tie the leaves round the bad leg and see if he could walk the dog home with him. There might be a few pence reward in it for him from the person who had lost it.

The stream was just a few steps away, and Desmond was soon down to the water and back with the sopping leaves.

When he got back, the sight that hit him shook him through and through. The dog had grown huge in the ditch. It was now as big as a bull, and its great red and white side heaved up and down. The whimpering

47

was now more like a howl.

The wet leaves froze his hands, and his eyes seemed to freeze with them. Then he knew he was trapped. He had been tricked by a Devil-dog. Oh yes, he had heard about Devil-dogs from Farmer Fidler.

"Devil-dogs…" Farmer Fidler had said, "they beg you to help them with their lame leg or their raggedy ear. You turn round and they've changed into Poison-fish or Blood-eagles, and you're a goner. Finished. Dead as old nails."

Desmond clenched his teeth together. "I ain't going to be beaten by no Devil-dog," he said to himself, and he stepped towards the giant beast.

Farmer Fidler had always said that if you ever meet a Devil-dog never say a word. Desmond would do just as Farmer Fidler said, but he reckoned he could do some-

*The wet leaves froze his hands, and
his eyes seemed to freeze with them.*

thing else. He'd beat this old Devil-dog with kindness.

With his hands shaking and his teeth held tight together, he tied the freezing leaves round the Devil-dog's leg. And not once did he say a thing. When the leg was all tied up, out of the ditch climbed the creature. It towered over Desmond and he could feel its warm breath on his face. It gave a husky "Ruff, ruff-ruff," right at him.

If I'm finished, now's the time, Desmond thought. At least no one can say I didn't try and help a poor dumb thing in pain.

Then, what do you know, the beast turned round and trotted off down the road away from Desmond.

"Well, what do you know," he said to himself. "What *do* you know! And didn't I see it wag its tail just then? But no one'll believe me when I tell that story later. But no matter, it's time I got home." And he took a good strong step towards home.

He hurried through the rest of The Tunnel and was soon heading down the part of the road he called The Snake. It curved first one way, then the other. Not long to go now, he thought, and he hurried on round the next bend.

But as he turned the corner, he came to a sudden standstill and jammed his legs stiff. In the middle of the road stood a huge, dark-coated goat, with bright green eyes and terrible hoofs and horns.

Desmond stared at it. Something in the back of his mind talked to him. Hadn't he heard once of a boy who was stopped on the road by a giant sheep and had turned and run screaming, and hadn't the giant sheep galloped right over him, crushing him with its giant hoofs? And didn't the people who

Desmond stood and faced up to the horrible goat.

told him the story say that the boy's terrible mistake was to turn and run? If he had stood and faced up to the creature he'd have been all right.

So Desmond did just that. He stood and faced up to the horrible goat. But, a moment later, it seemed like this was a frightful mistake, for the great goat took one look at Desmond and started to charge towards him with its head down, stamping the ground and roaring, its gleaming horns looming nearer and nearer.

"Now is the end," said Desmond. "Now is the end. But don't turn, Desmond boy, don't turn round."

Just then, from out of the hedge by the side of the road, leapt a huge red and white dog with a few old leaves tied round its leg. It was the Devil-dog.

It took a great pounce towards the goat

and landed on its back. Now the two beasts fought. Sparks flew up from the goat's hoofs on the road and the dog's teeth flashed. The only light on the whole scene came from the two animals' eyes. They roared and howled – the goat lunging at the dog with its horns and the dog trying to sink its teeth into the goat's neck.

Desmond knew what to do and what not to do. He took neither one step forwards nor one step backwards, but watched the whole fight with his legs still locked stiff. He could hear every breath and every grunt. It was terrifying but, even when it seemed as if the fight would roll right over him, he didn't move.

In the end, the goat was getting the worst of it, and it stepped away from the dog. But before Desmond could flicker an eyelid, there was no goat there. In its place flew an owl. It swooped over the dog, flapped silently past Desmond and away over the hedges and fields.

The Devil-dog stood panting, its great long tongue lolling out of its mouth like a huge lump of liver. It looked at Desmond, and a frightening growl came out of its throat.

Well, it's been a long time coming, thought Desmond, and now this is it. But deep inside that head of his, Farmer Fidler's voice told him, "Say nothing, not a word, not a thank you, not a sorry, not a good evening, not a goodbye. Nothing." He knew that if he did, that huge cave of a mouth would open wide and snap him up as if he were nothing more than a little bird.

But the great Devil-dog stood in his way, and Desmond had to get home. He couldn't stay here all night. If these beasts

No one looks back at a Devil-dog
and lives to see a new day.

didn't get him first, he'd freeze to death. So, without so much as an "excuse me" or a "please" Desmond walked first towards, and then past, the Devil-dog. It stayed just where it was until Desmond had left it behind him.

How he would have loved to look behind him. How he would have loved to glance over his shoulder to make sure he was safe, or to have one last glimpse of the great beast. But he knew not to. No one looks back at a Devil-dog and lives to see a new day. On he walked, on and on, and believe it or not, he didn't see another creature along the rest of the road that night. He never turned back all the way home, and never spoke of the things that happened that night to anyone at all – not even me.

Giant Gobbleguts was truly horrible,
and hairs grew out of his nose.

GOBBLEGUTS

Giant Gobbleguts lived in a cave and ate children. As soon as the children in the little village of No were big enough, Gobbleguts came raging down from the mountain, grabbed them, threw them into his Big Bad Bag and took them back to his cave. There he boiled them up in his great Stinking Stewing Pot and gobbled them down. He was truly horrible, and hairs grew out of his nose.

The last two children left in the village of No were twins.

"We're all alone," the two girls said to each other, "with no one to play with."

Flit and Flat, for those were their names, were still very, very small, but they knew that soon they would be big enough for Giant Gobbleguts. And if *they* knew they were big enough, then you can be sure Giant Gobbleguts knew too.

"Let's not wait for him to come and get us," said Flit to Flat, "let's go and find him."

Up the mountain they walked, towards Giant Gobbleguts' cave. When they were nearly there, they came face to face with him and his horrible hairy nose.

"Who are you?" he roared.

"We're Flit and Flat and we were looking for you, Gobbleguts," said Flit and Flat.

"Oh were you?" Gobbleguts said, and he reached down and put them in the Big Bad Bag. Then he turned round and marched back towards his cave and the Stinking Stewing Pot.

"Now, here's my dinner for today," he said.

The girls took no notice and played foggy-plonks in the Big Bad Bag. About half-way to the cave, Flit hopped out of the Big Bad Bag and started throwing stones up to her sister.

When the Big Bad Bag was full, both girls jumped out and ran away off home.

Gobbleguts got back to his cave and lay down to rest.

"When I wake up I will have dinner. Oh yes, yes, yes. Lovely juicy children for dinner."

He slept and snored for a day or two. When he woke up, he opened the Big Bad Bag and all he found was a heap of stones. He thumped the walls of the cave and wailed, "Waaaaaaaaaaaaaaaaaaa, I've been tricked!"

A few days later, Giant Gobbleguts came out of his cave and marched down the mountain. Flit and Flat came out to meet him and his horrible hairy nose.

"Now here's my dinner for today,"
said Giant Gobbleguts.

"Ah-hah. There you are girls, I was looking for you."

"We were looking for you," said Flit and Flat.

Once again he reached down, put them into the Big Bad Bag and marched back up the mountain towards his cave and the Stinking Stewing Pot.

"Now, here's my dinner for today," he said.

The girls took no notice and played knuckle-bashing in the Big Bad Bag. About half-way to the cave Flat hopped out of the Big Bad Bag and picked off a chunk of sticky resin that was oozing out of a tree trunk. Again and again she hopped out and ran from tree to tree until she had a great sticky load of it. Then both Flit and Flat smeared it all over the back of Giant Gobbleguts' jacket. When that was done, they hopped out and ran away off home.

Gobbleguts got back to his cave and lay down to rest.

"When I wake up I will have dinner. Oh yes, yes, yes, juicy children for dinner."

He slept and snored for a day or two, but when he tried to get up he found he was stuck to the ground. How he roared and shouted. The mountain shook with the noise of it.

"Waaaaaaaaaaaaaaaaa, I've been tricked!" he wailed.

A few days later Giant Gobbleguts came out of his cave again and marched down the mountain. Flit and Flat came out to meet him and his horrible hairy nose.

"Ah hah! There you are, girls, I was looking for you."

"We were looking for you," said Flit and Flat.

Once again he reached down, put them

into the Big Bad Bag and marched up the mountain, back to his cave and the Stinking Stewing Pot.

"Now here's my dinner for today," he said.

The girls took no notice and played nose-squashing in the Big Bad Bag. About half-way to the cave Flit and Flat hopped out and covered each other with mud. Thick, squelchy mud all over.

Gobbleguts got back to his cave and said, "This time I won't lie down for a rest first. That's how those two little devils tricked me last time. I'll fling them into my Stinking Stewing Pot right now."

And he did, and then lay down to rest.

"When I wake up, I'll have dinner. Oh yes, yes, yes, juicy children for dinner."

He slept and snored for a day or two. Inside the Stinking Stewing Pot the thick

"YEEEUURRCHH! Mud Soup!"

mud on Flit and Flat cooled the water down and kept them from burning. When the water was cold enough they sat in the pot scraping the mud off them into the stew. Then they hopped out and ran away off home.

When Giant Gobbleguts woke up he thought, wonderful Children Stew at last. He got the Stinking Stewing Pot bubbling and boiling and, when it was all hot and steamy, he dipped in his great big spoon and, "YEEEEEUUUUUUUUURRRRR RRRRRRRRCCCCHHHHHHHHHHH HHHHH!!!!! Mud Soup! Waaaaaaaaaaaaa, I've been tricked!" he wailed.

And that was just about as much as he could take of those tricky little twins, and he didn't come down the valley ever again to find children to eat.

*"Open up the door for your poor
old granny," called Old Greyface.*

OLD GREYFACE

Once upon a time in China there were three little girls called Seng, Ton and Po Ki. Seng was the oldest. One day their mum said, "I'm going on a long journey to see my mother, your grandmother. I won't get back till tomorrow morning, so Seng, you look after Ton and Po Ki. Stay in the house and don't let anyone come in."

Outside, Old Greyface, the wolf, watched the girls' mum leave the house. He waited till it got dark and then crept up to the door. Up he got on his back legs and tightened his throat to make his voice sound high. Then he knocked on the door and called out in a squeaky voice, "Open up the door for your poor old granny."

"But Mum's on her way to see *you*," said Seng.

"Oh dear," squeaked Old Greyface, "we must have missed each other on the way. Let me in girls."

"Your voice sounds a bit funny, Granny," said Seng, but Ton and Po Ki ran and opened the door.

In stepped the wolf and quickly blew out the candle, so the girls couldn't see him.

"Why did you blow out the candle, Granny?" asked Seng.

"The light hurts my eyes," said Old Greyface. Then he lowered himself down on to a chair.

"Ayeeeeee!" he screamed, for he had sat down right on his tail.

"*Ayeeeeee!*"

"What's the matter, Granny?" asked Seng.

"Oooooh, it's my back," said the wolf. "This chair's not very comfortable for me. I think I'll sit in your basket."

Old Greyface stepped over to the basket and dropped into it, exhausted from all this walking about on his hind legs. But as he dropped down, he let his tail flop into the basket after him – plomph!

"What was that noise?" said Seng.

"What noise?" said Old Greyface.

"That plomph," said Seng.

"Ah yes," said Old Greyface, "that's the chicken I've brought for your mother, dear."

Seng peered through the darkness. This wasn't Granny, she was sure. She thought quickly. Then she said, "Do you like nuts, Granny?"

"Nuts? What nuts?" said Old Greyface.

"Magic Yum-Yum Nuts!" said Seng. "Ooh, they're delicious. If you eat one, you want another. And when you eat another, you want another and another and another."

"Are they nicer to eat than little girls?" said Old Greyface.

"Oh yes, much nicer," said Seng.

"Where are these Magic Yum-Yum Nuts?" said Old Greyface. "I must have some."

"They grow on the tree at the corner of the house. I'll tell you what, Granny, you wait here, and we'll go and get you some of the Magic Yum-Yum Nuts."

"You never told us about them," said Ton.

"Shush!" said Seng. "Just follow me."

When they got outside, Seng said to her sisters, "Listen, it isn't Granny, it's a wolf."

"Listen, it isn't Granny,"
said Seng, "it's a wolf."

"Oh no, what do we do now?" asked Po Ki.

"Follow me," said Seng, and she climbed up the tree. Ton and Po Ki followed after.

Back in the house, Old Greyface waited and waited. In the end he went out to look for the girls.

"Where are you, girls?" he called out.

"Up here, Granny," said Seng. "These Magic Yum-Yum Nuts are so delicious. They're the sweetest, juiciest things you'll ever taste in all your life."

"Bring them down here," shouted Old Greyface.

"But Granny," said Seng, "these are *magic* nuts and the moment they leave the tree, they turn into wood. You'll have to come up if you want some, and bite them off the tree like we do."

"Don't tell him to come up here," said Ton, "he'll eat us up."

"Shush!" said Seng.

Poor Old Greyface. He walked and walked round the tree. He didn't know what to do. He couldn't climb trees.

"Your granny's too old to climb the tree," he said. "Show a little respect and kindness to your elders – come down here."

"Oh wait, Granny," said Seng. "I've got an idea. Back in the house, there's a long piece of rope. Bring the rope and the big basket you sat in, and we can pull you up to the top of the tree. Then you'll be able to eat all the Magic Yum-Yum Nuts you like."

By now the wolf was desperate to eat the nuts, or the girls, or both. He ran to the house and rushed back to the tree with the rope and the basket, in a trice. He threw the rope up into the air. The girls caught it, and then he tied the rope to the basket and climbed in.

"Come on, girls, pull me up!" shouted Old Greyface. He was so excited.

Seng pulled and pulled. Up went the basket. Up, up, up, till suddenly – flip! Seng let go of the rope. Down went the wolf and landed on the ground with a great WHAM!

"Oh, I'm sorry, Granny," shouted Seng. "I'm not very strong. Are you all right?"

"Oooh, my head!" said Old Greyface. "Listen, get one of your sisters to help you next time. Now pull me up."

Up, up, up went the basket, even higher this time, then – flip! They let go of the rope and down went the wolf again – WHAM!

"Oh Granny, I'm so sorry," said Seng. "The rope slipped through our fingers. Are you all right?"

"Oooh, my legs!" said Old Greyface. He was in agony, but now he was even

*Down went the wolf and landed on
the ground with a great WHAM!*

more desperate to get to the girls and the nuts.

"Listen," he roared, not bothering to sound like Granny any more, "PULL ME UP, all three of you, and *quick!*"

So now all three girls worked together pulling up the wolf in the basket.

"When you reach the top," called out Seng, "the Magic Yum-Yum Nuts will make you better."

"Now be careful this time," said Old Greyface. "If the basket falls, I'll gobble you all up."

Up, up, up went the basket, nearer and nearer to the girls. Up, up, up came Old Greyface. He opened his mouth wide – the girls could see every tooth in his mouth – when, *flip!* They let go of the rope again and down fell the wolf – WHAM! and this time he was dead.

When Mum came home in the morning, you can be sure they had a tale and a half to tell her.

Fokrul and Akhtar were on their way home from school. They took the short cut by the canal.

THE DUMP-DEMONS

Raymond Fenchurch used to sit over the Dump scaring other kids. He said there was a thing in the Dump called a Dump-demon. The Dump was out the back of the place where they broke cars up, and sometimes kids would go over there and pick up old wheels and things to make rockets and go-karts and contraptions.

One evening, Fokrul and Akhtar were on their way home from school, when Fokrul – who was the older brother – said, "Hey, why don't we go over to the Dump?"

They took the short cut by the canal, but it was blocked off. So they had to take a different way, round the back of the disused hospital. It was pouring with rain and, what with it being winter, it was very dark away from the lights of the street. Next thing they knew, they were lost.

"Where are we?" said Akhtar.

"I'm not really sure," said Fokrul.

"I'm tired," said Akhtar, "and it's dark. It's all your fault."

"OK, I know, I know," said Fokrul. "We'll stop here for a bit and get out of the rain."

There was an old workman's hut nearby, so the two boys went in. They stood by the door and watched the rain come down. Next thing they knew, they heard a strange scraping noise. It sounded like someone scraping bits of metal together.

"There's something out there," said Fokrul.

"There's something out there," said Fokrul.

Akhtar listened too.

There it was again, the strange scraping noise. What could it be? It didn't sound like a dustbin, more like a broken car.

Then a horrible, metal screechy voice said, "Smells like boys to me."

"Oh no," said Akhtar, "it's the Dump-demon Raymond Fenchurch was talking about. What shall we do?"

"OK, OK," said Fokrul. "I'll think of something. Just do what I tell you, OK? Go outside and stand by that old car wheel."

"No, I'm not going out there, *you* go."

"Listen, Akhtar, just do what I say and we'll be all right. I'll be coming out straight after you."

Akhtar went out shivering into the rain, and stood by the old car wheel. Fokrul followed him a few moments later holding an old iron bar he'd found in the hut.

Akhtar stood by the old car wheel, looking into the dark with the rain pouring down, while Fokrul went round the back of the workman's hut. Just then, up came three Dump-demons, their heads as high as lamposts, their bodies all greasy and rusty. They had only one eye between them. It was bigger than a bucket and glowed like the shop sign over the Nazrul café. They passed the eye between them, for each one of the Dump-demons had a hole in its head like the door of a washing machine where it put the eye and turned and twisted it about with its hands. It was a ghastly and horrible sight.

The Dump-demon who walked along first had the eye while the other two hung on behind. The first Dump-demon turned the eye round and saw Akhtar standing by the car wheel in the pouring rain.

"Ah-hah," it screeched, "I was right. It's a boy. Very tasty. I'll have that and grind him up in my mincers."

Akhtar looked up. Below the eye there was a great big hole with a door like the back of the dustman's lorry. It was opening and shutting with a roaring noise and dribbling some stinking juice or other. It took a great step towards Akhtar.

Just then Fokrul jumped out from behind the hut and gave one of the Dump-demons hanging on behind an almighty whack on the back of its leg with the iron bar.

"GAAAAAARG!" it screeched.

It was such a horrible, ghastly screech that the other two Dump-demons jumped with the fright of it, and the one holding the eye dropped it.

"Grab it! Grab the eye, Akhtar!" shouted Fokrul, and faster than a snake in slipped

"Gaaaaaarg!" screeched the Dump-demon.

Akhtar and grabbed the eye. How it glowed in his arms! When he looked into it and through it, he could see everything in the dark just as if it were day.

Now the Dump-demons didn't know what was going on.

"What dented my leg?"

"Where's the eye?"

"Hell's bells! Find the eye!"

"You've got the eye, haven't you?"

"No, you have."

"No, *you* have!"

"I've got the eye," shouted Akhtar.

"And it was me that dented your leg," shouted Fokrul. "And we're from the Bradbury Flats."

"Oh ho!" shouted the Dump-demons. "Nothing can save you now. We will fling you from the top of the high-rise block on the corner of the Mile End Road, and when you hit the ground you will break into little bits. And then we'll put you in our crunchers and your bones will snap like matchsticks. Our crunchers will grind you up to oily gravy."

"You're just a bunch of rusty old Dump-demons," sneered Fokrul. "We've got five eyes and you've got none. We're fit and fine but one of you is hobbling about on a dented leg and the other two'll have to carry him. You're about as much use as a car without an engine."

"Oh you little pin-heads," screeched the Dump-demons. "If you don't give us back our eye, we'll turn you into tin cans and squash you flatter than a sheet of paper – till all your insides are outside."

"You threaten us with any more of that bad talk," said Fokrul, "and I'll whack all three of you so hard you'll be worse off than broken bikes."

"No, no, no," said the Dump-demons, trying to make their screechy voices as soft as they could. "Oh no, little boys, such lovely little boys, we were only teasing. It was all in fun, little boys. But please, little darlings, give us back our eye and all will be forgotten. We will give you skateboards, racing bikes, Porsche 5000s – anything just to have our eye back."

"How many?" asked Fokrul.

"Squads of them," said the Dump-demons.

"You'd better bring those skateboards and racing bikes and Porsche 5000s right here, then you can have your eye back."

Oh, how the Dump-demons screeched and scraped now. They clanged their tanks and rolled on the ground. They screeched so loudly that their Dump-demon wife heard them. A great rusty old thing she was,

*Their Dump-demon wife
was a great rusty old thing.*

and she screeched at them from over by the Dump.

"Now what's the matter, you big ninnies?"

"A little thing no bigger than a gas cooker has stolen our eye and won't give it back till we give him our squad of Porsches."

"Then crunch the little gas cooker thing, jump on it and squash it," screeched back the Dump-demon wife.

"You do that, and I'll squash your eye!" said Fokrul.

"He says he'll squash our eye," shouted the Dump-demons. "Just bring us all the Porsches and the skateboards and the racing bikes we've stolen. Now!" wailed the Dump-demons.

So along came the great rusty Dump-demon wife, dragging all the cars and bikes and skateboards behind her.

"Now where's the little gas cooker thing?" she screeched. "By all the iron in the Blackpool Tower I will turn you into a bent pin."

"Oh shush, Wife, shush," whispered the Dump-demons. "Shut your cruncher, or they'll smash our eye and dent our legs."

"Just leave the stuff there," said Fokrul. "Quick Akhtar, jump into that Porsche, chuck some skateboards in the back and let's go."

"What about the eye?" shouted Akhtar.

"I'll show you!"

With one huge heave, Fokrul flung the glowing eye up into the air, over the Dump and into the canal, where it sank to the bottom. For a while you could see it glowing down there until it slowly fizzled out and everything went dark again.

*And they zoomed home faster than
a laserbeam can cross a street.*

"Your eye's gone that way," shouted Fokrul.

"What way?" screeched the Dump-demons.

"The other way!" shouted Fokrul and Akhtar. And they both jumped into the Porsche and zoomed home faster than a laserbeam can cross a street. And they had never driven a car before in their lives!

You can imagine what a story they told Raymond Fenchurch the next morning at school. He doesn't go down to the Dump any more, I can tell you. And the Dump-demons haven't been seen there either.

THE

END